The Catacombs

Collected by Raven Black

The Catacombs

Collected by Raven Black

An imprint of Gauthier Publications

Gauthier Publications
P.O. Box 806241
Saint Clair Shores, MI 48080
Attention Permissions Department

Cover Photo: Daniel Gauthier
Editing: Merideth Hadala
Book Design: Elizabeth Gauthier
This is a work of fiction. All characters in this book are
fictitious and any similarities are coincidence and unintentional.

1st Edition
Hungry Goat Press is an Imprint of Gauthier Publications
www.EATaBOOK.com

ISBN: 978-06922467-2-6

Table of Contents

Vacant

Careful now do not speak.
Listen closely the stairs do creak.
Not foot but hoof bends ancient wood,
try and run it will do no good.
Time travels at a different pace
inside the aging walls of this place.
Something happened once before,
behind the cracked and broken door.
The same one now you hide behind,
easy you will be to find.
A bloody moon full and red.
An older woman now you instead.
A poor place to hide,
a childish dare to make.
Coming here was your last mistake.
A disappearance famous for years,
you remember now, shed your tears.
Whereabouts unknown, no witness found,
only monsterous tracks upon the ground.
A vacant home left to decay,
waiting for you until today.

Raven Black

Three Sisters
by Charlotte Birch

There were three beds in the rectangular, low-ceilinged room. Each bed was occupied by one of three sisters. The middle eldest, Rebecca, lay in the middle bed and stared up at the ceiling. She'd willed herself to relax, for her mind to at long last switch off and for sleep to consume her; but like so many previous nights she stared open-eyed at the dark silhouettes of the room, sleep a far off luxury.

Sighing she moved her head to her right and made out the long blonde curls that cascaded down the quilt of her younger sister, Maggie. Her deep-breathing sounds seemed to increase in volume until they seemed to echo in Rebecca's head. Wrapping her pillow around her ears Rebecca tried to block out the sound and the world but it was no good, sleep wouldn't come.

Rebecca turned her head to her left and made out the straight, dark locks that sprawled out down the quilt like spider's legs of her older sister, Candace. Rebecca watched as Candace fidgeted around under her cover, kicking out her foot and thumping her arm free.

The sounds of Candace's fidgeting seemed to increase in volume until the noise became too much for Rebecca. She cupped her pillow around her head and tried to block out the room, only it didn't work.

Accepting her sleepless fate, Rebecca lay there wide awake as the sky started to lighten and the birds began their chorus.

It had started a week ago, this not being able to sleep. Before then she'd never met a problem, not once. She'd usually been the first sister to fall asleep and she'd slept straight through Maggie's deep-breathing and Candace's endless fidgeting.

She'd always shared this room with her sisters, it was her familiarity. Yet now, everything about it seemed alien.

She didn't tell anyone about her problem, not even her sisters. She knew what they'd do: they'd tell Harriet. They'd think that they were helping; they wouldn't understand how Harriet knowing would only hinder things.

Finally as the brightness of morning had begun to dominate, Rebecca fell asleep.

'Rebecca, wake-up,' Maggie said, as she pulled off Rebecca's cover with over enthusiastic energy.

'Not again, Rebecca. You're going to get us into trouble with Harriet,' Candace said, as she stood by her bed, re-positioning her cover.

Rebecca forced herself to sit-up and swung her legs over the side of her bed. Rubbing her eyes, she yawned and outstretched her arms, dropping them by her sides in a lapse of energy.

She carried on as if on auto-pilot, staggering around the room as she made her bed and got dressed.

***

The three sisters sat around the rectangular wooden table, a vase containing three white lilies was positioned in the middle of the table. They all wore identical white dresses with a piece of black satin tied around their waist and they each wore a ribbon in their hair. Maggie wore a yellow one, Rebecca's was red, and Candace's blue.

They waited in silence as they always did until the sound of the gong. On hearing this sound, Maggie pushed her seat back and walked out of the room. She returned a minute later, with three bowls full of thick, steaming porridge and three glasses of tomato juice balanced on a tray. She placed it down on the table and each sister reached for the bowl and glass closest to them.

Once finished, Maggie piled the empty glasses and bowls onto the tray and carried them out of the room. Candace stayed where she was, tapping her fingers on the table to an unheard tune.

Rebecca's eyelids felt so heavy, she tried to resist closing them but the temptation became too much.

At first she remained confused as to what was happening, then she realised she was being shaken and there were familiar voices. As she opened her eyes, Candace stood in front of her, her hands clasped around Rebecca's shoulders. Maggie was by her side and they were both speaking, words that began to un-blur and start to make sense.

'Wake-up, you're going to get us into trouble,' Candace said.

Rebecca apologised as she forced her eyes to stay open. The sisters went back to sitting quietly and waited until the gong sounded. On hearing the noise, they all pushed their seats back and stood up at the same time. Maggie started to walk towards the door and the others followed.

***

The weather was placid; it wasn't cold as such, but nor was it hot. The three girls sat cross-legged on a tartan rug by the pond near their house. Maggie loved to watch the ducks that sometimes visited it, although she no longer snuck out food for them; not since Harriet had found out.

Rebecca used to like sitting by the pond and reading; she'd loved losing herself in the works of fiction. Harriet had found out though and put a lock on the library door. In her eyes fiction was a means of hiding and one should only live in reality. Still, Rebecca found the pond relaxing even without a book.

Her sisters knew what Candace was doing when she tried to make secret glances over at the trees beyond the pond. She was looking for the blonde-haired boy, even though he hadn't appeared in months. Harriet had most likely scared him off; she'd made it very clear what she felt about the perils of boys.

Rebecca often wondered what it'd be like to leave the house and the garden and run off into the trees. She knew it was dangerous to think like this; their house was safe whereas life beyond those trees wasn't. Maybe Harriet was right and books were bad things that corrupted ones imagination.

Maybe they were the reason she could no longer sleep.

The sisters remained on the rug, too scared to venture off it. They looked curiously at their surroundings and they each became lost in their own thoughts. Rebecca's mind fell easily into wonderment, but she remained in enough control of her own mind to stay awake. If anything, she feared sleep. It'd been so long since she'd slept properly, she was worried that when sleep next eventually took her over, that no amount of shaking or shouting off her sisters would wake her up. She didn't want to never wake up; she didn't want to become a lost soul.

Candace was the first to step off the rug. She straightened the creases out of her dress and reached out a hand to Maggie before helping to pull her up. Maggie begged for Rebecca to join them but she merely shook her head. Knowing how stubborn their sister could be they left her alone. Candace proceeded to close her eyes and count aloud as Maggie ran off giggling in pursuit of a hiding place.

Candace walked across the grass. As she neared the edge of the trees she slowed down, she was well aware that Maggie would never hide here but she had to check by the middle tree in the front row. It was then she saw it, weighed down with a large stone and half-hidden under leaves; it was a piece of crisp, white paper. Picking it up, she quickly folded it and then slid it into her shoe before carrying on her search for Maggie.

'You can't hide from me,' Candace said in jest. 'I'm going to find you.'

It was Maggie's laughter that gave her away and Candace soon found her, hidden beneath the bridge that ran across the stream.

Out from under the bridge, Maggie put her hands over her eyes and started to count aloud. Candace didn't trust Maggie not to peek so she decided to run off in the opposite way to which Maggie was standing. On deciding to hide behind a bush closer to the house she took her shoe off and acting as if she had a stone in it she shook it, whilst carefully removing the folded up paper in her other hand. With her shoe back on and making sure her hunched over body hid the paper from anyone's view, with sweaty fingers she unfolded it and scanned her eyes over the written message: Meet me tonight, by the entrance to the trees.

'Candace, I'm going to find you,' Maggie's nearing voice shouted.

Candace ripped the note into as many pieces as she could before hiding them in her closed palm as Maggie's footsteps grew closer.

'Got you,' Maggie said, as she crept up behind her sister and placed her hands on her shoulders which caused Candace to jump.

As her sisters sat back down on the rug, Rebecca didn't let Candace know that she was aware of what she was trying to do when she searched for Maggie that close to the trees. They both knew full well that Maggie would never go that close; she knew her sisters would go mad at her if she ever did. She'd been careless, what if Harriet had seen?

The gong sounded and the sisters fell silent. They all knew their time outside was over for the day and they all stood up in unison. It was as Maggie folded up the rug that Candace strolled over to the pond and dropped the bits of paper into the water, not waiting around to watch as the water claimed the note as its own.

Maggie led the way inside, clutching the rug to her chest. Rebecca walked in the middle of the line and Candace at the back until they were once again in the confines of the house.

***

That night, once again Rebecca found that sleep wouldn't come. Her mind was tired and her whole body felt exhausted, yet she just couldn't fall asleep.

Looking to her right she made out Maggie, deep breathing beneath her quilt. The sound seemed to multiply in the average sized room until it was all she could hear.

Looking to her left she made out Candace, only she wasn't fidgeting, instead she was still. Rebecca knew that Candace was never still for long when she was sleep so that meant only one thing, she was still awake.

Rebecca closed her eyes and feigned sleeping. It wasn't long before she heard a sound to her left, it sounded like a cover being moved back, followed by footsteps.

Rebecca opened her eyes to make out the silhouette of her elder sister walking towards the door. At first she thought she'd imagined it; Candace wouldn't leave the room at night, she knew it was forbidden. Yet as Rebecca saw Candace tiptoe across the room and slowly open the door, she knew it was real. Candace disappeared beyond the security of their room and Rebecca was left to stare her sister's empty bed.

She thought Candace would come back, she had to come back. Rebecca's thoughts were interrupted by a single high-pitched scream. It hadn't woken Maggie, she carried on deep-breathing in her sleep as normal, but Rebecca knew what she'd heard and she couldn't just lie there anymore.

Pulling her cover back Rebecca stepped out of bed and hesitated before walking across the floor. She'd never stepped out of bed at this time before and it felt unnatural doing so, yet she forced herself to keep on moving. The floor creaked beneath her feet and she stopped still. Harriet was sure to know, Harriet knew everything and then she'd be in trouble, big trouble. Rebecca knew she couldn't turn back, she'd heard a scream and her sister was missing; she had to check it out.

She took her time to carefully open the door and walk out into the corridor. The first thing she noticed was how creepy it looked in the darkness; it was somehow haunting and no longer felt familiar. The only sounds were of her breathing and the beating of her heart which was so loud she thought it may fight its way out of her chest. Clutching onto the banister she forced herself to keep on moving.

It was as she walked further along the corridor that she saw it on the wall to her left; it was a hand print, made in blood. A trail of blood was trickling down the magnolia wall. Rebecca turned around and she ran back along the corridor and back into her room.

Back in bed she tried to convince herself that she'd imagined it and that Candace was fine. Even though she was afraid she couldn't stop her tired eyes from flickering shut and even through the horrors of the night, she soon fell asleep.

***

Rebecca awoke to Maggie desperately pulling at her covers.

'Wake-up, wake-up, it's Candace, she's gone,' Maggie said.

Rebecca instinctively turned her head to her left and looked at the space where her sister's bed had once been, only now it had gone. The only proof it had ever been there were the darker shaded wooden floorboards marking out where her bed had once been.

'I don't understand. Where is she?' Maggie said, her voice full of panic.

'She's gone,' Rebecca replied, stepping out of bed and beginning to make it.

Maggie understood what Rebecca had meant and even though she had lots of questions she wanted to ask her, she knew better than to do so. She paused for a moment to collect her thoughts before continuing to get ready.

***

The two sisters sat around the rectangular wooden table. A vase containing three lilies were positioned in the middle of the table, two of which had paper white petals and looked freshly picked but the other lily's petals were shrivelled-up and blackened.

Neither of the sisters dared to look at the empty space where Candace had once sat. There was no seat there and no placemat set out. To Maggie it felt as if she'd never had an eldest sister, as if she'd never existed. Rebecca knew different though, her mind still had a vivid imagine of the fresh bloody handprint dripping down the wall.

The two sisters sat in silence until the gong sounded. On hearing it, Maggie pushed her seat back and walked out of the room. She returned a minute later with two bowls full of thick, steaming porridge and two glasses of tomato juice balanced on a tray. She placed it down on the table and Rebecca took the bowl and glass closest to her.

When they'd finished, Maggie piled the empty glasses and bowls onto the tray and carried them out of the room.

Rebecca waited for her younger sister to return, her eyes fixed on the door. As Maggie came back into the room and sat down in her seat, Rebecca found that the sickening feeling in her stomach had at least to a degree subsided.

The two sisters sat in silence until the gong sounded, then they both pushed their seats back and Rebecca followed Maggie out of the room.

***

The two sisters sat opposite each other in the large windowsill, both hugging their legs close to their chests as they looked out of the window at the bleak weather. The fierce raindrops thudded against the glass with unforgiving menace.

Maggie found herself missing Candace, she always used to hug her during storms and reassure her there was no need to be scared. Rebecca didn't comfort her, instead she rubbed the back of her bare arm across the steamed up window and stared out at the darkened sky as if it was enchanted. Placing her hand against the cold, damp glass she dared to let her tired mind wonder upon Candace. Maybe she'd made it and maybe she was out there?

Rebecca had read in books of how love could be potent but she had thought nothing of it, she'd never been in love so she hadn't understood why Candace was so drawn to that boy. All Rebecca knew of love was through her books but this was fiction, it was only now as she stared out of the window at the eerie, grey world that she realised even fictional books came with warnings.

***

The bedroom didn't seem complete; there seemed to be an unease to it which polluted the air and caused Rebecca to once again remain wide awake. Maggie was asleep, she could hear her deep-breathing noises but still she turned her head to her right to check that she could still make out the silhouette of her younger sister beneath the covers.

Turning her head to her left she took in the space where Candace's bed had once been but there were no sounds of fidgeting or sight of her sister's long dark hair.

The first signs of morning began to dawn, the birds chirped and light streaked through a gap in the curtains and illuminated the space where Candace's bed had once been. Eventually as the time to wake up came ever closer, Rebecca fell asleep.

***

The two sisters sat around the rectangular wooden table, a vase containing two white lilies was positioned in the middle of the table.

Both sisters sat in silence until they heard the sound of the gong. On hearing this, Maggie pushed her seat back and left the room. She returned carrying a tray with two bowls of thick, steaming porridge and two glasses of tomato juice and placed it on the table. Each sister grabbed the bowl and glass closest to them and ate their breakfast in silence.

When they'd both finished, they placed their empty bowls and glasses onto the tray and Maggie carried it out of the room.

Rebecca waited anxiously for her sister's return and found herself feeling more at ease when Maggie walked back into the room and sat down in her seat.

They both waited for the sound of the gong. On hearing it, Rebecca followed Maggie out of the room.

***

The two sisters sat cross-legged on the tartan rug that was on the dew-splattered grass. Although the garden was still showing signs of yesterday's storm, Rebecca could feel the sun warm against her skin. She made sure she remained on the rug, knowing how angry Harriet would become if she messed up her dress.

Rebecca strained to keep her eyes open but this was a task she was failing; she could no longer keep her mind awake. As long as she didn't miss going in time or fall off the rug, she decided that no harm could come from resting her tired eyes.

Maggie was finding her sister boring. Rebecca just sat there with her eyes closed, so Maggie decided to find her own entertainment; she decided to explore.

She walked carefully around the pond, studying the damp, leant-over long grass that sprouted out in clumps around the pond border and she crouched over to look at a ladybird that was making its way over a pebble. She loved how vibrant red their shells were and how tickly they felt when crawling along her outstretched finger. She also found amusement in attempting to count the amount of spots they had on them before they flew off.

Everyone had a weakness in life, or as Rebecca liked to phrase it an Achilles's Heel; a saying she'd got out of a book. For Maggie, her weaknesses were creatures; from the smallest ladybird to the largest duck, she found them all fascinating.

She first saw it at the opening to the trees, rubbing its fur up against a tree. She loved cats, especially their eyes. When she was a little girl, her mother told wonderful tales about cats and how their eyes lit the way in the dark and had saved lives. Maggie didn't remember much about her mother so the cat story had given her an extra fondness for these creatures. Harriet made it very clear they would never have a pet and that animals should be left to their own devices.

Candace wasn't here to tell her not to be stupid and Rebecca looked like she was asleep, so Maggie decided no harm could come from going up to the black cat and stroking it.

Hearing her feet squelch across the grass and being careful to lift the hem of her dress, Maggie walked over to the edge of the trees and slowly edged closer to the cat as she reached out her arm.

The cat purred and threaded itself through Maggie's legs, causing her to laugh. Suddenly the cat froze still, pricked up its ears, and then started to run off into the trees.

'No, come back,' Maggie said, running off after it.

Surrounded by willowing, intimidatingly high trees she soon felt small, like a doll taken out of its dollhouse and forced into the real world. She couldn't find the cat and she was lost in a forbidden place. The panic set in as she found herself running in a frenzied scurry.

'Rebecca!' she shouted, 'Rebecca, please help me, please find me!' words that were claimed by the trees.

She didn't see the twig and she tripped, bashing her knee against a sharp-edged rock. The blood oozed out of her cut, streaked down her leg and seeped through her dress. She was in so much trouble; she was lost and she'd ruined her dress. She started to cry. At first she tried to sniff back the tears, but then she decided to let them fall down her cheeks.

When Rebecca finally opened her eyes it was to the sound of a single high pitched scream. It took her a moment to adjust her eyes to the light and realise where she was. Maggie? Where was Maggie?

She desperately scanned her eyes across the garden but there was no sign of her younger sister. That was when she saw the handprint on one of the middle, front trees; it was fresh and made out of blood. It was still damp; she could make out some of the red substance trickling down the bark.

The gong sounded, Rebecca picked up the rug and folded it up before making her way back into the house.

***

The bedroom looked bare without her sisters' beds in it and as Rebecca lay in bed unable to sleep, she found herself automatically looking to her right and her left desperate for her sisters to magically appear and tell her this had all been a nightmare; one brought on by sleep deprivation.

She'd never been in the bedroom alone before, it seemed too big for just her. To a degree it felt like her sisters had never been here at all and she worried that over time she'd forget about them.

She had no concrete proof that either sister wasn't still out there. All she'd seen were the handprints and she couldn't fully assume the worst, although she knew Harriet and she knew how much she hated being disobeyed.

The room's silence was too peculiar to Rebecca. It felt like she was in a new room, one that was unfamiliar, and this added to her anxiety. She wanted to sleep and join her sisters in dreams about her past but she just couldn't. It was only as morning was beginning to dawn that Rebecca finally fell asleep.

***

Rebecca found that although sleep-deprived she still woke up at the normal time. She got ready, went downstairs and sat behind the rectangular wooden table with a vase with one white lily and one black, rotting lily in it positioned in the middle of the table.

The gong sounded and for a horrible moment Rebecca didn't know what to do. It was always Maggie that went and got the tray, not her; it wasn't her job because she wasn't the youngest. Letting her mind ponder, she realised that it didn't matter what aged sister she was because she was the only one left. There was no one else to go and get that tray.

Pushing her seat back she walked out of the room, along the stark, dark corridor and pushed open the kitchen door. There was no one in the medium-sized, neat kitchen. Rebecca's eyes fell on the tray that was on the square oak table in the centre of the room. There was a bowl of steaming, thick porridge and a glass of tomato juice on it. Walking up to the tray, she picked it up and held it out-stretched, trying her best to balance it.

Back in the other room she ate in silence and on the sound of the gong she took the tray back into the kitchen.

Everywhere was too silent without her sisters, she felt completely alone. There was no one to talk to or just to look at for reassurance. It was just her now, just her. Suddenly the notion of never waking up from her sleep seemed somehow appealing; what was there to wake up to?

On the sound of the gong Rebecca left the dining room, picked up the tartan rug by the door and started to make her way outside. As soon as the slight wind brushed the morning air against her face she realised something; something that caused her to drop the rug and run back inside and up the corridor until she reached the library. As she banged her fists against the black locked door, she realised that she had nothing to lose.

Running into the dining room she picked up the one chair that was placed around the table and swung it forwards so that the vase with the one alive and one dead lily smashed to pieces. Carrying the chair she made her way back up the corridor and swung the chair into the black door.

Kicking at the door she fought her way into the library, not caring that splinters from the doorframe embedded in her arm. She stood there, her arms scratched, and she looked a fierce mess; yet she was surrounded by books, hundreds of books. It was there that she forgot about the recent chaos and became lost in the enchantment of the variety of book covers and the smell of paper.

Rebecca grabbed a book off a huge, pine shelf and ran out of the room, along the corridor and up the stairs, until she got into her bedroom. With every bit of strength she could find she started to push her bed so that it blocked the doorway.

As she crouched in the corner of the room she began to read.

The first thing she heard was the footsteps; but she ignored them.

The next thing she heard was the banging; but she ignored it.

They were in the room now with her, stood in the doorway looking over at her; yet she continued to read.

Rebecca dropped the book to the floor and sheltered

herself with her arms as the knife was stabbed at her. She begged them to stop but they continued until her hair became matted with her own blood and her white dress was stained vivid red

The stabbing stopped and Rebecca desperately reached out a blood-stained hand and touched it against the wall.

The yank on her legs caught her off guard and she let out a load, lingering scream as she was pulled along the floor. Her arms fell limp and her eyes started to flicker shut; the last thing she saw was the handprint, her handprint, and her blood trickling down the wall.

One week later

The three girls stood on the doorstep of the grand house and stared up at the door with apprehension and curiosity. They didn't know why they'd been brought here; to them nothing seemed to make sense.

Beckoned, they hesitantly stepped inside and the door closed behind them.

They were told to look upon each other as sisters and that they would be safe here as long as they obeyed the rules.

The Red Rooms

A. Gregg

Dan had always wondered why you sometimes saw rooms that were red. He'd presumed it was because they had red curtains that let the light through, or a red lightshade, or perhaps even a red light bulb. So when he knocked on a neighbor's door one day, with a parcel that had been mistakenly delivered to his flat, he felt pretty stupid on realizing that it was hell.

He then felt even more stupid for being in hell and his initial thought being 'Oh, that explains the red.' The sequence of stupidity was abruptly curtailed by a demon ushering him in, taking the parcel and closing the door behind Dan. He turned around, knowing already there would be no door. There was no door. He wished he hadn't checked.

He appeared to have no choice but to follow the demon down the hallway, avoiding the licking flames that went for walls around those parts. The demon turned and scowled at him. "Ain't you been allocated yet?" the demon asked.

"Er, I don't think so," Dan replied.

"Well, what did you die of? What are your sins?" asked the demon, glancing at his wrist where there was no watch. Time wasn't needed here, but the demon, being a demon, innately went for gestures that conveyed that whoever he was talking to was wasting his time.

"I don't think I'm dead," said Dan, slightly annoyed by his ability to sound apologetic even when trapped in the eternal embers of evil.

"Oh for crying out loud!" snarled the demon. "In there," he pointed to a room, red of course, and continued walking away.Not knowing what else to do, and considering it unlikely that following the demon would have any productive effects, Dan entered the red room.

There was a chair, old oak and high back. Dan looked nervously around the room and, not fancying sitting on the floor carpeted with small flames, sat on the chair, rested his forearms on the armrests, and waited. He wondered why the chair wasn't on fire, knew at the same time that the chair wasn't just a chair but was a representation of all the old wood; the slow, sturdy life that had survived millennia.Dan waited some more. At some point he noticed how straight he was sitting and wished that he could see his Mum one last time to tell her how his posture had improved and make her laugh. He was certain now that there would be no more seeing his Mum or laughing. Dan waited to find out what was going to happen to him. After a while he realized that he wasn't obliged to sit in the chair, and got up. He turned and saw that through the haze of the heat there was a window. He peered and saw his flat across the way. It felt like he was dreaming of a place he'd lived once, years and years ago. He reached his hand out towards his old home, pulled it back when it hurt from being too hot. Dan sat back in the chair, and waited. And waited. He remembered the saying that hell was other people. He yearned to be given the opportunity to compare for himself. He rued not remembering who was responsible for the quote, and all the other things he'd never bothered to make a point of knowing.

Eventually he got up. He left the room and wandered down the hallway. He noted that this flat had the same boiler set-up as his. It occurred to him that maybe he could turn the heat down, make hell fade away. He looked for the temperature dial; felt his heart sink as the temperature rose as he saw that the dial was a melted clock face. Like in a picture by that bloke, the one with the 'stache. If only he'd made the time to gather knowledge, to be interested in the arts, maybe he would have learnt from others valuable information to help him out in his time of need. Tears fell from his eyes and evaporated before they reached his cheeks.

He continued down the hallway, in the direction he'd seen the demon going all that time ago. He pushed open the door of where his bedroom would have been, not caring if it burnt him. It didn't. He was mildly disappointed to not have something dramatic to distract him from the monotonous passing of heavy time.

There was no bed in here; but there was a demon, crouched over a huge fire burning in the middle of the floor. The room was lined with small books of street maps, and the demon was surrounded by parcels. Dan stared, wondering if the demon was moonlighting, or firelighting as the case must be, as a postal worker.

"Can I help you?" asked the demon in a cold tone that was at odds with their surroundings. There were many things Dan could have asked, and many things he should have asked; but he wracked his brain and couldn't think of any of them beyond his terrible confusion.

"Why have you got so many street maps and parcels?" Dan asked feebly. The demon ran a gnarly finger down the index of a street map that was next to him, looked up a page, checked it against the address on the parcel nearest him, and tore out the page. He threw this and the parcel on to the fire, and turned slightly to Dan.

"Got to make sure there's an even distribution of annoyance, inconvenience, and distrust, ain't I?" said the demon.

"But why throw people's parcels away in the first place?" asked Dan.

"You stupid or something?" the demon replied. "For fostering an atmosphere amongst the civilians of the world of annoyance, inconvenience, and distrust. What else do you think we do with the fires of hell if not burn stuff? Make ickle wickle fairy cakes for the kiddies?"

Dan looked evenly at the demon. It was one thing being trapped in hell for no apparent reason, but it was quite another to be openly mocked. "No," said Dan as haughtily as he could. "I did not think that. But I did presume that you would be doing something more impressive than stealing people's post."

"Oh you did, did you? Well I'll tell you something for nothing my man. No need. We just have to create a brooding resentment that people don't even realize is there, and they do all the rest for us. All your raping and murdering etcetera etcetera, all your acts of petty vandalism that make other people feel like it's too much effort bothering to make life nice: that's all down to people wanting to feel like they have a bit of power, just for a moment, because we've made them feel worthless, and like their fellow human ain't worth nothing either."

"People aren't like that," said Dan, but quietly. He was remembering all the times he'd wanted to throw things at too-fast motorists in the hope they'd swerve and crash and die; and when he'd wanted to shout at boring blokes in the pub for having the cheek to not be to his liking; or tell women to put some clothes on because they dared to have bodies that weren't like his; when he had ranted and raved about the inefficiency and corruption and downright inhumanity of the everyday. He marveled that he'd never lost his mind; wondered how long it would have been until he did if he'd remained in the world; suddenly sympathized with his fellow humans that had cracked and gone wrong and been everything he'd been disgusted by and never thought he could be.

The demon had got on with his task of checking addresses and chucking parcels in the fire. "What's that one?" asked Dan.

"Book from an estranged Dad to his young son to show he's still thinking of him," replied the demon.

"And that one?" asked Dan as the demon reached for the next parcel, the next representation of someone wanting someone else to feel special.

"A cheap mug," said the demon, "sent from a daughter to her mother to remind her to make time to relax and enjoy."

"Why are you- why is all this- why are you here? Opposite my flat?"

"Nothing personal. Just where this particular room of hell is"

"But why? Why are there even rooms of hell?" Dan asked desperately.

"Gotta have rooms of hell haven't you? Where else you gonna put hell?"

"I thought it was... you know... below."

"Below what?"

"Oh... The Earth?"

"Earth's floating in space pal, use your brain."

"Then where's heaven?" Dan asked eventually.

"Anywhere else, obviously."

Dan just had time before hell successfully broke his heart to think of all the times he'd been in heaven and not known it. He wished in his last moment that he could feel incredibly stupid again, before icy sadness washed his thoughts away.

Darkness Falls
Steven Spellman

THE OCEAN WAS RELATIVELY CALM. The sounds of wave after wave softly crashing against the shore, the white froth speeding up the shore a short distance before retreating back into the water, was soothing, calming. A complete ruse. An unlikely trio, two guys and a girl, lounged upon the edge of the beach near the water, watching the surf. One of them, one of the guys, sat off a little from his two buddies while they kissed and fondled each other, losing themselves in each others mouths and under each other's clothes. Clara wore a bikini top embroidered upon the straps and edges in Pez candy pieces. Her bikini bottom would've been covered in candy pieces as well except that Ralph had discouraged her from wearing panties tonight so she wore nothing beneath a short pink skirt.

She leaned over, making out with Ralph, now. Her hips were tilted at such an angle that Sean could see the neat creases at the bottom of her buttock clearly beneath that short skirt. A voice, a hope really, in the back of his head told him that the view was on purpose. He sat sullenly in the sand, his knees pulled up to his flat chest, his thin arms holding them there. "You know, you guys should really get a room," he said, staring out upon the ocean.

"And you should really get a girlfriend," Ralph answered once he could reclaim his tongue from Clara's mouth. Sean only scoffed. "Haven't you heard the saying, three's a crowd?" Sean scoffed louder.

"Well, look," Sean said, rising to his feet "I'm gonna take a walk,"—his tone said clearly that he would've rather not—"and leave you two lovebirds alone."

"Good idea," Ralph mumbled from somewhere in Clara's face.

Sean hobbled on down the edge of the shore, only stopping every now and again to kick sand and mumble about the fact the Clara should've been his girl. Ralph treated her like a prostitute as far as he was concerned and she was just too blind to realize it. He was kicking an increasingly deep hole into a patch of sand when he noticed that the waves were crashing more violently nearby. Nothing alarming, but as he watched the froth cover his feet where it had not before...yes, not only were the waves coming in further, but the water was warm, almost uncomfortably warm. It was nearing the end of autumn. Winter was approaching and the cool temperatures were the only reason he and his two horny companions could sit on the beach alone without flocks of tourists mulling about in every direction. The water was always cooler this time of year but now it was quickly becoming too hot for Sean to remain in the surf.

The waves were rising higher and higher and when they crashed now it was with a strange sound, like the muffled groaning of some great dinosaur. Sean hadn't noticed it before but out upon the horizon was a lone surfer. Sean could barely make out the silhouette of the man. He only noticed him because of his large bright yellow surfboard. Probably some tourist that didn't realize the Season for Strangers was over for the beaches of Nags Head, N.C. The surfer seemed to be racing against the huge waves until one so large that the crest rose dozens of feet above his head rolled in and swallowed him up. Literally; when the wave crashed there was no sign of surfer or bright board.

The sun was almost fully set now and the waters seemed to be growing more agitated the more the sky dimmed. Sean scanned the horizon for the missing surfer until finally he decided that it was time to return to his friends.

Ralph and Clara were still kissing and groping to the tune of their own moans and groans when Sean arrived. "Man, I think somebody is out there drowning," he said, not sure if he should panic, not sure if he had seen what he thought. The moans and smack of wet lips continued on unabated. "I'm serious. I think something is wrong out there!" he was beginning to panic.

"Then go sit in the car. We'll be there...in a while." Sean turned and gazed back out into the ocean. His breath was coming quicker than he would've liked; he would be panting soon. The crashing of waves was so loud now with that strange sound that Ralph and Clara finally looked up, both of them. Only the very tip of the sun was peeking out over the waters now. It would be full dark very soon. They were both laughing at first but as they continued to stare out over the 30, 40, 50 foot and rising waves, they began breathing faster too. They both jumped to their feet and shuffled further inland a short distance. That was when Sean noticed that the waters came inshore only so much no matter how the waves crashed. He could see steam rising from the froth now and feel the heat; the ocean was boiling; but still the waters only came inshore to a specific point, as if something more palpable than the sand was discouraging their progress.

"What's that?" Clara asked, pointing, mouth agape, out onto the ocean. Sean raised his eyes and saw that a great dark spot like a massive oil spill was moving closer to shore. The darkness spread out in every direction, a huge circle of blackness so dark that it was clear to see even in the moonlit gloom of the now set sun. Everywhere this growing darkness spread it instantly stilled the raging waves, making them recede at its edge, a huge circle of empty air in the midst of what was rapidly turning into a full blown tsunami. The darkness continued to spread until it rolled onto shore instead of water, leaving no white froth in its wake. It too came only as far as the water had, held back by some invisible force. From way out in the center of this 'oil spill,' figures began to emerge from its murky depths. No one could tell exactly what the figures were, only that they rose from the blackness like corpses from an opened grave and then began lumbering upon its surface toward the shore.

It was only as the first figures drew closer that the trio could see skeletons; some missing skulls, some missing hands, arms, some stumbling along on the ends of flesh-less ankles where feet should've been, every one of them in varying states of decay. There were also non-skeletal men and woman, bloodless flesh falling from their bodies with every step like dead leaves from a shaken tree, every one of them with ragged gaping holes where their faces should've been. There were animal shapes too—only shapes, out-lines as black as pitch—of lions and tigers and bears, some of them with the heads of eagles, some with the heads of woman with long flowing tresses. These began to lumber along the surface of the blackness as well, spreading out over the ocean. No matter how near they came they never grew more distinct; impossible shadow puppets.

The trio watched on. Terror like nothing they'd ever experienced rooted their feet in place. Not until it was clear that these horrible aberrations were all intent upon reach-ing the beach, upon reaching them, did the spell break and they ran. Clara's screaming was like the screeching of a cat. They turned tail and ran so fast through the cool sand back to Ralph's car waiting at a pier entrance nearby, that they didn't notice that something else was also forming from the spreading blackness. A huge distorted face, as large as a small home, rose from the middle of the massive ink blot, drawing up the blackness in its ascent as a person would draw water upon their skin rising out of a pool. The huge face was more of a mask, pale white with small cracks spreading and receding everywhere but especially outward from the eyes; where the eyes would've been if the face had any. Instead, there were only empty holes, as black as the abyss on either side of the face's nose. Not empty holes—the abyss itself. The crown and temples of the face were as smoke, constantly drifting up and dissipating into the moonlit night but never lessening the headless facade.

Its gaunt cheeks and loosely drawn lips betrayed no emotion as it hovered above the ocean. The blackness from which it had risen flowed from it like the many skirts of a Victorian-era dress. The massive face turned slowly toward where the trio was still running. Only then did the lips draw up and in a hideous grimace; or perhaps a smile.

RALPH WASN'T SCREAMING LIKE CLARA, but as he fumbled for the right key to unlock the driver's side door of his car, he looked as if he might start matching her hysteria at any moment. "Shut up, Clara!" he exploded as he dropped the keys for the third time. He snatched them up and began fumbling again; he was too panicked to even consider slowing down long enough to find the right key. Clara's yelping only rose in pitch.

"Ralph!" Sean demanded. "Ralph, hurry up!" Ralph looked up toward the beach and saw what all the fuss was about; the hobbling skeletons were close, less than a hundred feet away. There were not as many of them as had emerged from the blackness, and the other aberrations, the shadow animals and rotting corpses, were nowhere to be found. They were already headed off in other directions. Other...things were steadily emerging from the blackness as well. The blackness itself may've been held at bay at the beach's edge but its terrible offspring were not. Ralph threw the keys at the car and raised his hand as if he would punch out the window and say to hell with the locks, then thought better of it. Perhaps he was concerned about breaking his hand or maybe it was the fact that the skeletons would be upon him and his friends within seconds. Either way, he turned and ran as fast as he could. Sean and Clara looked on, dumbfounded. They didn't look long though, before they followed closely behind.

With Ralph in the lead, the three ran to the nearest house: a large two story rental property surrounded completely by a chest-high old rickety wooden fence. Ralph leaped upon the fence, careful to not impale himself on the decorative spikes, and was nearly over it before Clara and Sean got there. Sean was shorter than Ralph but he scaled the fence as well, scrambling across the top like a large child. Clara came last and knocked the wind out of herself when she jumped and landed nearly squarely on one of the blunted wooden pikes. She couldn't yell for help and Ralph was already scouting the area for somewhere to hide. Had not Sean looked back to make sure she was still following, she would've likely remained upon the fence until one of those awful things came and tore her apart. Sean called for

Ralph but he was already around a far corner, cowering in a corner of the fence. He was peeking fearfully through some of fence's leaning boards to make sure nothing was coming his way. He was concerned with nothing else. Sean leveraged himself upon the fence and tried to pull Clara free but her tiny skirt was caught upon the tips of two of the spikes.

Clara yanked at the skirt but it wouldn't give. Finally, Sean heaved back with everything he had and luckily her entire skirt didn't come off upon the spike, but a jagged bit of fabric did. Even more of the firmly toned thigh of her left leg was exposed now and Sean couldn't help but ogle as she ran barefooted to find Ralph. He didn't ogle long.

He understood that he wouldn't live long standing around like this. He rounded the corner after Clara just as Ralph was yanking her down beside him. "Shut up, Clara, or so help me God I'll throw you back over that fence!" Clara wanted to know how he could just abandon her like that, but now she sat silently, lips tightly sealed; after what she had seen she had little doubt that Ralph would make good on his threat, girlfriend or no. Sean dropped down with his friends as Ralph glared at him and Clara. Clearly he didn't like sharing his hiding spot. There was no sign of the skeletons and after a while everyone began to notice that there was another sound in the air. It was the sound of moans and heavy breathing that wasn't from fear. Ralph was the first to turn to the nearest window of the house. The shades were drawn up and circles of softly colored lights danced across floor, wall, and ceiling. Someone had some a strobe light running. It took a moment for his eyes to focus and when they did Ralph was still not sure he was seeing correctly.

In the room behind the window, in the middle of the floor surrounded on every side by all manner of strange and oddly shaped erotic toys, sat a thick wooden table. Secured to this table was a woman, completely naked except for the thick layers of leather straps that bound her ankles and wrists to the legs of the table. Metal combination locks made sure she would not escape the straps until the man looming over her released her. The man was covered head to toe in purple spandex. Only his nose and mouth showed through the tight glossy fiber. With his left hand he held a wad of the woman's hair, pulling her head up, and with his right hand he assaulted her exposed bottom with a thin wooden paddle. Apparently he was berating the woman, and by the look on her face, the way her eyes rolled into her skull, she was enjoying it a great deal. Ralph couldn't make out what the man was saying but he could hear the muffled pop every time that paddle met flesh.

Ralph was still watching when the man turned toward the window. At first he thought that he and his two friends had been found out but suddenly the man was not yelling but screaming. It took awhile to tell what was going on, but soon Ralph, Clara, and Sean could all see that the man's shadow was actually raising itself from the floor. The shadow stood now, as tall as the man, in front of him as if it were its own body. A black hand gripped the man's head and slowly squeezed until his skull gave way and brain matter and blood began to ooze from the face opening in the purple spandex head gear. The black hand squeezed until its fingers were lost in the crushed skull, then it let the body drop heavily to the floor like so much worthless baggage. The woman was thrashing wildly against her restraints now. The shadow melted back into the floor and the woman's own shadow rose in its place. Her shadow wrapped black arms around her middle, sliding in between her and the table, and slowly pulled her body taut against her restraints. The woman continued to thrash until her arms straightened completely, and the flesh covering her joints began to tear. Ralph couldn't hear it but his mind added its own sound effects as he watched the woman's left arm separate at the elbow, her right arm at the shoulder, both her legs at the knees. Blood spurted everywhere, a sickly brown syrup in the circles of light rotating about the room. Her shadow held her up, still alive, mouth wide in silent agony; a body nearly as ruined as the walking corpses from earlier. The shadow slowly squeezed the woman's middle, squeezed until ribs imploded, squeezed until the woman's waist was no larger than either of her dismembered wrists and thick green bile bubbled from her mouth. Then her shadow simply let her body drop to the floor beside the man, before melding itself back into the floor.

"Aaaahhhhh!" the sound of Clara again screaming at

the top of her lungs startled Ralph so badly that he was on his feet and preparing to flee again before he realized that he wasn't in immediate danger. Ralph normally enjoyed the fact that Clara was a screamer. Not tonight.

Sean rose to his feet. "We got to get out of here!" No one protested and even Ralph followed as Sean, bent nearly double so his head didn't rise above the spikes of the fence, headed for the fence's dilapidated door. He tried to be cautious, tried to open the door without it squeaking, but it was old, the hinges nearly rusted through. It was only halfway open before one of those hinges gave and the door fell sideways—loudly—and hung there swinging—and squeaking—at an odd angle, holding on by only the bottom hinge. Sean craned his neck trying to look in every direction. He was sure all that noise had attracted attention—the wrong kind of attention. And to his horror he found that it had. Not far off, on the side of the narrow two lane 'Beach Road' that ran in front of the house, Sean could barely make out two shadowy figures like goats with the stubby legs of pigs and the heads of lions, feasting on what he was sure had once been a living person. The figures weren't shadowy they were shadow; when the two figures turned their heads toward him they were nearly two dimensional.

One of the animals growled at Sean then immediately lowered his head down to the mangled pulp beneath it that had been a person, sunk its black teeth into the ugly mass of flesh and bone that had once been a head and flung the corpse aside like a discarded chew toy. The thing wanted lunch out of the way so he could make Sean and his friends his late night after meal snack. The trio began running again, running for all they were worth, running for their lives. Sean didn't want to the run the length of the highway—he had enough sense to know that he probably couldn't match the speed of these animal things, even with their stubby legs—but he was not about to dart in between the rental houses and be mired in the sand. His bare feet protested against the grainy pavement but he never slowed his stride. He ran and ran until he felt like his heart would give out and then he continued running. At last he risked a look behind him, to make sure that his two friends, but especially Clara, were still in tow. They were, but they were both doubled over a few feet behind, gasping for breath.

The animal shapes—how strange that shapes, shadows of things could devastate so completely; David probably never walked through the valley of these shadows of death—were no where in sight. The street lights lining the road were not nearly close enough for Sean's liking—those animal shadows could be lurking anywhere it was dark—but he could tell from the spots swimming before his eyes and the painful throbbing in his chest that he would pass out if he didn't catch a breath. He didn't think it was wise to stop, not for a second, but if he passed out there was a great chance that he would never come to again on this side of death's door. He was just beginning to regain his breath when he noticed movement from the corner of his eye. Something very large was moving in the dark areas between those street lights. Something huge that would've eclipsed all else had it been any closer. In the interspersed light it was impossible to tell what it was—nothing friendly, no doubt—only that it was moving toward Clara and Ralph. It drew closer and seemed to grow larger with every lumbering step. Then there was more movement, shadow against shadow, directly above Ralph's head. As far as Sean could tell something was being raised. His head rose with the movement and then whatever it was was brought back to the ground with a slow speed that bespoke something truly massive making haste. It wasn't until Ralph was smashed to the ground, bent double the wrong way like some hideous contortionist, that Sean recognized the shape to be an elephant's foot; with a shadow elephant larger than any real elephant connected to it.

Sean snatched Clara's hand and began to run again, harder this time. Neither of them stayed to watch the elephant scrape a foot upon the pavement in an effort to rid itself of Ralph's smashed remains, as a man would grind dog droppings from his shoe. The only thing left of Ralph now was a brief, viscous stain upon the pavement. Meanwhile, neither Sean nor Clara looked behind them to see if they were being followed. They ran past homes and rental properties, most of them vacant but some of them filled with the screams of dying men, women, children, which spilled out into the streets like so much vomit. It only made Sean run harder. But he couldn't run forever, he needed a place to hide. The idea of being indoors where he could be cornered brought bile into his throat, but remaining out in the open where anything could close in on him from any direction brought the icy grip of terror upon his spine. He had an idea. He ran with Clara to the other side of the road. Where he planned to go, where he hoped to go, was not far away. Before many moments had passed it came into view—a Sonic burger joint. He had worked there before, maybe a year earlier, and he remembered how well lit and secure the walk-in freezer was. He ran to the back of the building and—thank God!—the door was open.

It was still operating hours and the store had been staffed earlier, but that was before everyone had abandoned it, running and screaming, from every sort of odd terror the darkness seemed to be producing tonight. From the back door, Sean craned his neck in every direction to make sure nothing was following. Nothing was following— not yet—but he noticed that something substantial was keeping the dumpster lid nearby from closing completely. Immediately he wished he hadn't noticed it: a body draped over the edge beneath the lid and lip of the dumpster like an old curtain. As Sean entered the building and slammed the heavy door shut behind him, the body fell to the ground. Or rather, only half a body. Some unfortunate soul had been torn apart from the waist down, made literally half the man other men were.

The freezer was as cold as Sean remembered, colder for Clara in her candy embroidered bikini top and torn miniskirt. But more importantly, the freezer was very well lit. The ceiling was permeated with large powerful bulbs that flooded the room in light that would've been way too bright on any other night besides this. Every corner, every box, all three large metal assortment shelves, filled with everything from frozen bags of fries to chili beans; everything was lit from every angle, nowhere for shadow to hide. "I need to make sure nothing's inside the store," Sean told Clara, who was already beginning to shiver.

"No, don't leave me! Please, don't leave me!" After having Ralph abandon her as he had it was no wonder that she was terrified.

"I have to, Clara. I have to make sure we're safe in here,"—he really did; the store doors could be locked but there was no way to lock the freezer's heavy metal door from the inside.

She thought it over for a moment, her shivering quickly escalating. "O-o.k," she sighed at last. "But come back! Please, come back! Don't leave me here!"

"I won't," Sean promised; a promise he fully intended to keep. "I won't leave you Clara..." it was an effort not to add 'like Ralph did.' As Sean peered down into Clara's eyes for emphasis, he had to restrain himself from taking her into his arms and not leaving the freezer at all. He wanted Clara, had always wanted her, and perhaps even loved her. But she was—had been—his friend's girl and so she had al ways been off limits. "I promise I'll be back,"—he also did not add 'if I'm still alive' though he thought it—"as soon as

I'm sure we're safe. I promise." The relief upon Clara's face was clear.

Sean had already locked the back door, all that remained was to check the building and lock the two front doors on either side of the restaurant's lobby. He moved up and down the aisles in the back, to the manager's office, to both condiment stations, to the fryers and grills; everything was clear. He looked quickly and carefully over the lobby as he locked the doors. His heart pounded in his ears and his breath was mist in the cold night air. The bathroom was the scariest place to check, closed in as it was. He stared at the door for a long time. His mind reminded him needlessly that this was a door that once he entered, he may never exit. He did enter it, reluctantly, because his mind also reminded him that either way he would probably not make it out of this alive. Heading back to the cooler he gazed out into the night. The distant screams of victims of the night, the disembodied howls and yelps of animals never meant to walk the earth, bled in through the glass of the lobby. Sean was almost certain that if he listened closely enough he would hear the tearing of flesh, the shattering of bone.

When he opened the door to the freezer, he found Clara huddled in a corner between two of the metal shelves. Her legs were huddled to her chest in a pitifully futile attempt to conserve warmth, and tightly grasped in her hands was an opened bag of frozen jalapeño poppers. Shaking terribly from the cold she reached into the bag and grabbed a frozen popper as soon as she heard the creak of the freezer. She looked as if she were about to hurl it until she looked up, teeth chattering, and saw that it was Sean. So, she had meant to protect herself with projectiles of frozen foodstuffs? Sean could've cried to see the woman he'd pined for for so long in such a pitiful state. He dropped to his knees and enfolded her in his arms. He covered her as much as he could with his body until he could feel her shivering subside, if only a little. They remained like this for a long time, silent, always listening for another creak of the door, a creak that would mean their doom more than likely, as the hours passed slowly by. Clara was warmer than before, if not exactly comfortable, enfolded in Sean's arms and legs but his embrace was becoming looser. He had been rubbing her back as well, anything to generate warmth, but his gentle circular motions upon Clara's back were becoming less and less. He moved less and less in general. It wouldn't be long now before he stopped moving altogether, lulled by the freezing temperatures into a deep sleep. He was literally freezing to death trying to keep Clara warm.

He must've realized that as well. "C-Clara, we h-have to get o-out of h-here." She could not answer; her lips were chapped beyond feeling and she couldn't move them. It was as if they weren't her own anymore. She could only nod her head slowly and only with the greatest effort. Sean dislodged his arms from around her slowly and stiffly. He couldn't feel anything: arms, hands, legs, feet—everything was as numb as a prosthetic limb. He wobbled to his feet awkwardly. It was a struggle to maintain his balance, what with the total lack of sensation. He supported himself on one of the racks of the nearest metal shelf and remained there, unmoving, until Clara thought that maybe he had fallen asleep anyway. Eventually he did move, to lift a heavy arm slowly into the air. He did it again. Then again: more quickly with each attempt. He raised a leg, then again, the same way. He stood on his own and moved the other arm. Then again. He jumped a small distance off the floor and nearly toppled over but grabbed the rack in the nick of time. He jumped again, then again. He was doing full jumping jacks now and the color was quickly returning to his otherwise ashen brown cheeks. He reached down and helped Clara to her feet. It took a moment, but before too long she was doing vigorous jumping jacks as well.

After a while they finally stopped, both of them panting and sweating.

"We need to get out of here, Clara." She only looked into his eyes blankly. She lacked the heart to ask where they could possibly go, what they could possibly do.

"I need to get to Ralph's car."

"No, Sean! Don't!" Clara pleaded. In her head, she could still see Ralph being bent double and smashed like a large bug.

"I have to, or you'll die here." It did not escape her that he hadn't said 'or we'll die here.' She found it simultaneously odd and sweet and he was more concerned with her survival then his own. She fell upon his neck and hugged him tightly.

"Stay here with me," she whispered into his chest.

"I'm gonna come back for you, Clara. I promise. If it's the last thing I do, I'm gonna come back for you." He raised her head and kissed her lips so quickly that she was not certain it had happened. Then he was gone, slipping through the freezer before she could protest. "I'll blow the horn three times at the back door. When you feel yourself getting sleepy do jumping jacks...promise me."

"I...I promise," Clara answered and Sean slipped out and closed the heavy metal door.

THE COLDNESS OF THE NIGHT was warm compared to the conditions in that storage freezer. Sean ran through the short side streets to reach Beach Road: the narrow road he, Clara, and, for a short time, Ralph, had run to get to the restaurant. He was craning his neck this way and that so fast that he nearly lost his balance more than once, trying to watch in every direction at the same time for any imminent threat. There were moving shadows, unnatural figures, hideous animal hybrids, and other things off in the distance seemingly everywhere, tearing, ripping, gnashing; but for whatever reason none close enough or interested enough in him to give chase. Still, he never lessened his breakneck stride.

He was closer to where Ralph's car was, though not within immediate sight of it. A cop car, the lights atop it flashing furiously, straddled the street at an awkward angle. Sean could see that the driver's side door was opened and that a figure of some sort was hanging from the seat onto the pavement. When he drew closer he noticed the figure was moving. It must've been a trick of the pole light nearby but there was blue of a police uniform here, then there, as if someone were moving a flashlight across the body. The officer was obviously hurt but he was still moving, so at least he was still alive. If Sean could help him maybe he could receive some help in return. When he closed in on the officer he noticed that the figure's movement was odd in the extreme. It was eye wrenching. It looked as if the officer were writhing as a snake would, but not quite. The officer's entire facade was shaded more than it should've been and his slumped body quivered with a certain graceful fluidness that human bones would've never permitted. It was with a start that Sean realized that what he was seeing was not the man's writhing but a thick carpet of black maggots covering a corpse. They twisted and squirmed everywhere, sometimes gathering together enough to show a patch of partially destroyed uniform here, then here, throughout the length of the body. Nothing besides these momentary patches was visible because of their thick coverage.

Sean vomited before he could stop himself and immediately a mass of the black maggots rushed into the disgusting spew until it was as covered as the fallen officer. Many of maggots were turning to flies instantly before Sean's eyes. These instant flies quickly surrounded Sean, collecting upon his arms and legs, struggling to crawl their way upon his eyes, into his ears. He bolted and just barely escaped the cloud that was forming around him. He decided that he would not stop again, no matter what he saw. He made it to Ralph's car and breathed a deep sigh of relief even as he bent low to snatch up the keys that were still lying on the ground near the driver's side door. He looked around; still no imminent threat, not yet. He tried to listen for anything unseen that may be approaching, but he could hear nothing over the sound of his own pounding heart. Still, he couldn't afford to make the same mistake, out of frustration, that Ralph had. He needed to find the right key and in order to do that he needed to calm himself. With an effort greater than anything he'd every mustered, he slowed his frantic breathing and forced his hands to slow their shaking enough to sift through the keys. After an eternity he found the right one, abandoned calm, and leapt into the driver's seat. He raced down the street, carefully avoiding the still flashing cop car, and was at the rear entrance to the Sonic in record time.

He hit the horn. He hit it again, longer. He hit it again, holding it down, a blare long enough to wake the dead; as if worse things weren't already awake. He waited. No sign of Clara. He hit the horn another three times and began to grow more uneasy at how loud the sound was, how easily it could attract the wrong kind of attention. Still, no Clara. He looked around, flung the door open and then, with a grunt, flung himself out of the car and bounded for the restaurant's back door. He flung that open and found Clara on the other side, her hand on the knob but shivering so hard that she couldn't turn it. Her brown skin was showing a slight bluish tint. Frostbite was setting in. He snatched her up into his arms—Sean had always secretly admired Clara's curvy hips and full breasts, but just now those curves came with a weight that he wouldn't have been able to carry had not his bloodstream been saturated with adrenaline—and lumbered to the passenger side of the car. It was difficult trying to open the door and look around at the same time without dropping Clara, but somehow Sean accomplished it. As soon as they were both safely in the car, he turned the heat up as high as it would go until Clara stopped shivering and her full golden brown hue began to return.

They were flying down the highway now, the main highway, without a care for speed limits or other cars that may suddenly dart out from any of the many side streets. Sean continued speeding, with no plan of where to go; only that he couldn't stop until the sun began to peek over the horizon. Morning had come at last. Not only was night receding, but the strange shadows and the many other aberrations with it. It would seem as if morning had brought with it his and Clara's salvation. "I think it's gonna be all right, Clara," he said cautiously. He didn't know if things were going to be alright—he certainly hoped so—he was just trying to ease Clara's mind. She leaned over and gave his cheek a long kiss, the best kiss he had ever had as far as he was concerned.

"Thank you." It was simple but it said everything. "I think it will be alright."

THE CREEPY MASK-LIKE FACE continued to loom over the blackened waters, gazing out upon the shore, watching the dire destruction its children had created. The smoky face of death with its empty—not empty, bottom-less—eye sockets and expressionless façade turned slowly, with the speed of a great behemoth, to the east where, just as it turned, the sun was beginning to peek across the horizon. The huge face turned back to the beach as broken skeletons, shadow animals of every size and shape, things that looked like vivisection gone horribly wrong, and every unholy thing besides, walked, lumbered, slinked, and flew to the blackness straddling the shore and coming in with the tide. They all made their various ways upon the surface of the blackness and when they had all arrived, the huge face opened its thin pale lips as if to draw in a breath; and with that 'breath' it absorbed all its creatures back into it-self. Then it too lowered back into the blackness and the blackness itself began to recede back from whence it had come. But not before those waxy white thin lips pulled up into a hideous smile. Perhaps it anticipated its return the next time darkness fell.

Dancer in Oblivion
J.B. Williams

My name is Megan. I killed the world. Well, not the whole world. Just all the people. It was an accident. But things are better now. Calm and quiet and no one left to hurt me.

And I inherit all that is left.

I am the last.

Almost every day, I make the trip to the dance studio, biking the twelve blocks past all the empty row houses. Their yards have grown unkempt, weeds sprouting up in gleeful unchecked spread, vines beginning to cover walls and creep over shingle-shedding roofs. I've been in most of them, raiding them of canned food and books and DVDs.

The studio is very quiet; the kind of silence that presses on my ears, probably because of the cork insulation Madame Willis had put on the walls a few weeks before The Event happened. Some of the people on the floor below had complained about the noise of classical music and thumping feet. No one will be doing that again, I guess.

The window in the west wall looks out over the gray river and across at the gray skyline of downtown. I turn the blinds so the sun isn't so bright.

I stretch a little - the bike ride is sufficient warm-up - put on a red leotard, tie pointe shoes, and turn the music on. The electricity still works, yes. That puzzled me, till I remembered the hydroelectric dam outside of town. As long as the river flows and the CDs hold up, I have music.

I turn Tchaikovsky up as loud as I want. I take all the space I was never allowed to have before; light streaming in through the window making slanted spotlights across the room, my figure flitting before the mirrors lining the walls, each showing an identical reflection, all of them moving in perfect unison and time.

Pirouette.

Arabesque.

Plié. Plié. Plié.

It was partly Dad's fault.

I feel bad about Dad. He was a great guy, even if he did act like a cartoon mad scientist every time he tried to invent something. I never really understood exactly what it was he did for the government. "It's so top-secret, I can't even tell you," he used to say, right before he'd pretend to steal my nose and wiggle his thumb between his fingers with that loony grin on his face. I used to think he was joking about the top-secret part, but now I really wonder.

I used to feed the gerbils and the mice in the basement where Dad had his workshop. Clean the cages, too - Dad was supposed to do that, but he always forgot. If I didn't do it the whole house would start to stink like mouse pee within a couple of weeks. Dad was never big on practical details like that.

I came down the stairs with a plastic bag full of pine shavings for the little rodents' cages that night, about a week before The Event happened. Dad hadn't locked the door. He was hunched over the table, running his hands over this gray box with lots of little buttons. He jumped a little when he saw me come in, and then he smiled the biggest cartoon-mad-scientist smile.

"What's going on?" I asked. Ordinarily I knew better than to ask for details about whatever he was working on, but this felt different. He looked sort of like his head might explode.

Dad patted the little box, and then motioned for me to sit down on the wobbly chair next to his. His face turned very serious, the scary kind of serious.

"You have to promise not to tell anyone," he said. "I could end up in the federal pen if you did. It's gonna be a national security matter."

I promised. Who am I going to tell, Dad? I've got no

friends, in case you didn't realize. Not that I could say that to him, or tell him about all the things the girls in dance class did. It was outside his comprehension. I didn't want to go into it anyway.

Dad picked up the box. He pressed the orange button, then the yellow one, and then looked over at the racks of cages.

"See that gerbil there?" he asked, and pointed.

It was a brown and white one, running endlessly around its wheel, making it give the tiniest of repetitive squeaks.

Dad held the box up a little, so it was pointed vaguely in the gerbil's direction. He closed his eyes. "I'm thinking of that gerbil. Just that particular one."

He waited a moment, and then pressed the blue button, without opening his eyes.

There was a strange, pressing feeling in the air. A bending sensation, almost, and a very faint popping sound like soap bubbles dissolving.

The gerbil turned wavy and indistinct in mid-stride. Then it was gone.

I dropped the bag of paper shreds. The wheel kept turning a few more times, then squeaked to a stop.

I remember staring at Dad, open-mouthed like a little kid on Christmas morning. He was grinning again, like that same kid after it dives into the presents.

"What is that?" I whispered.

Dad put the box down and put his hands on my shoulders.

"That, Meg," he said, "is the ultimate weapon. And it's going to make us rich."

Poor Dad.

It really happened because of that little witch Bianca Rahm. You know the type. Perfectly blond, blue-eyed, and thin. Long corn silk hair and the ability to eat anything she wanted and never gain an ounce. In leotard and pointe shoes, she had the grace of a butterfly; skimming effortlessly across the dance studio's polished floor in dead-accurate leaps and pirouettes, the mirrored walls reflecting back a score of equally perfect mimicking reflections.

She had the most silvery little giggle. I heard it, faintly among the music or behind Madame Willis' counting out of beats, every time I took the floor on my own. Compared to Bianca, my pirouettes were wobbly, jumps stumbling, arabesques the laughably awkward flailing of a rhinoceros leg.

Just having someone in class so perfect that I wanted to punch her in her concave mannequin-model stomach every time I saw her was painful enough. That faint giggling whenever I galumphed around the studio was worse. But nothing too bad could happen out on the floor, because Madame was there.

She wasn't there in the dressing room, where I heard the grunting moo and oink sounds from Bianca and her little friends as I changed. Madame wasn't backstage at recital rehearsals, where I'd smell the faintest hint of the jasmine perfume Bianca always wore right before her manicured fingernails dug sharply into my side or the back of a thigh.

Madame wasn't at the studio on time that one day, so she didn't witness Bianca shout, "Hey, guys, this is Megan dancing!" and her flopping, arm-flapping, hooting clump across the floor... the ridiculous, broken-puppet images lurching identically in the mirrored walls' depths...the laughter of the other girls.

I sat cross-legged in the corner, staring at the grain of the wood in the floor. I never spoke up. What would have been the point? If you speak up, it only encourages them. I'd learned that from the way the other students treated me at school. This wasn't different from anything that happened to me there.

But then, two weeks later, Bianca and her friends went too far.

The end of the world ended up being caused by the mother of one of my fellow dance students. Mrs. Hayes, I think her name was. We'd just finished class when she came in and waylaid Madame, talking urgently about something-or-other in low tones. If it hadn't been for Mrs. Hayes, maybe Madame would have noticed the commotion in the dressing room, maybe stopped the other girls from what they did, or kept me from leaving for long enough so I didn't go home and...

We all clomped wearily into the long, low dressing room. The fluorescent lights flickered overhead. There was a funny smell: faint, vaguely like biology class.

I should have noticed that the chatter was much less than usual, that Bianca and her friends didn't make any animal sounds while I was opening my locker.

They were watching, you see. Waiting for my reaction.

I opened the locker, and the biology-class smell poured out in a rush.

My clothes had been taken out of my bag and torn to pieces, piled on the locker's bottom. The rest of the locker's insides were splashed with whipped cream and shredded jelly doughnuts. Something sickly white and stinking dangled by a string from the hook on the back wall. It took a moment to realize what it was: a fetal pig, pickled and grinning, its tongue hanging out.

I screamed, more out of surprise than actual fear.

Rising laughter and Bianca's voice, right in my ear: "What's the matter, PIG-an? You're not scared of a member of your own family, are you?"

I turned around just as two of the other girls came up on either side of me. I got one quick glimpse of Bianca's smiling little face before her friends grabbed my arms and threw me, sending me stumbling forward and falling over one of the benches onto the polished tile.

The others advanced. I only looked up once, long enough to see the cans of whipped cream and chocolate sauce in their hands, and the wickedly sharp high-heeled shoe in Bianca's.

After that, I was too busy covering my head, feeling the sticky crap landing on me, absorbing kicks and punches and the blows of that shoe, hoping they weren't breaking any bones. I don't know why I didn't scream. The idea felt as futile as fighting back against all eight of those girls would have been.

By the time they got tired and trooped out, still laughing, I'd scuttled under the same bench they'd thrown me over. It took a while to get the chocolate sauce out of my eyes. My leotard was gaudy with chocolate and bloodstains. I flexed my legs cautiously. My pink tights were covered in rips from Bianca hitting my legs with the shoe, the skin beneath already bruising in livid red dots.

I didn't bother getting anything out of my locker. I just carefully got to my feet and crept out the door, breathing through my mouth, snorting whipped cream and blood out of my nose.

Madame was still talking to Mrs. Hayes. They must have heard my approach, because they both turned as I walked across the studio floor. Madame's mouth fell open, a perfect O of shock.

"Megan! What on earth -"

I ran down the stairs, out into the sun-bright street, for home.

I couldn't keep running for very long. It hurt too much. I slowed to a walk, limping and numb, heart frozen and everything around me reduced to a weird sort of tunnel vision and hearing. Drivers slowed and stared curiously as they passed me. I barely noticed. I just kept hearing Bianca's voice, hearing that gaggle of girls laughing.

Dad's car wasn't in the driveway, and I knew from the quality of silence in the house that he wasn't home. I walked down the basement stairs, shaking all over.

He'd left the workroom door unlocked. Just like Dad, to build a weapon with implications for national security and then leave it unsecured while he went to get bread and milk. The gerbils were squeaking their wheels and the room smelled faintly of rodent pee again.

The gray box was on the table, surrounded by a scatter of screws and gears and crumpled technical drawings with fast-food grease stains on them.

I sat down, very carefully.

I picked up the box, very carefully.

I pushed the orange button, then the yellow.

I began to think of Bianca...and poisonous dark red hate

welled up inside, so intensely that it blotted out everything. Not just hate for her, or the other girls. Hate for everyone who'd ever done or tried the same on me, hate so thick that it blotted all the images and thoughts from my mind and left only darkness and an internal scream for destruction.

That was when I pushed the blue button.

The air shivered and rumbled, as with a distant earthquake deep in the ground. The pressing, bending sensation that followed was so heavy that it knocked me down against the table and made my vision distort. The pop after that drove bright spikes of pain into my ears and head with its volume, and everything went gray for a long while.

When I awoke, I was the only human being left on Earth.

After practice, I ride my bike a few miles west, across the bridge into downtown. It feels odd, even now, to not lock the bike up once I reach a place I want to explore. (Theft doesn't exist anymore; we now have a completely crimeless society, ha.)

In some streets, it's easier going without the bike. Rafts of shaggy bushes spring up through cracks in the pavement in some places. In others, especially alleys and the little side streets, the way is choked with fallen shingles and window glass. Main Street is clogged with abandoned cars, some in the middle of the road.

I like to sit in the big gazebo overlooking the lake at the park, sometimes. I always have to find a stick and knock the bird crap off the seats first. The pigeons and starlings build nests in scores in the rafters now, with no one to scare them off. The fountain in the middle of the lake stopped working last year, and the water now swims with thin dark weeds and the amazing number of ducks that come to eat them. Most of the park grounds are waist-high in grass, and the flowers have burst their beds, their colors riotous in the green.

The main city library is two blocks away. I always enter through a back service door that someone left unlocked on the day of The Event. Something in the works of the automatic front doors jammed, and they won't open now. It's not as nice a place to be as it was before. Even though the AC still works, there's a green stench of mold in the air, decay creeping in through vents and around the vine-darkened windows. I went walking the stacks two years ago, going through the entire collection with a cart and pulling out everything I might possibly want. The books are piled on the main circulation desk downstairs, a couple hundred of them.

Just for fun, I beep my card at the only circulation desk computer that still works, and check out six books, which go into my backpack. I keep thinking I'll get up the energy someday to push Dad's old wheelbarrow all the way here and take the rest of these books, so I don't have to come back. Ever since I was in the children's section and found that dropped rag doll in the stacks, I don't like it in here. I didn't like the way the thing's eyes looked, shiny and blank and eternal, staring up at me. It's still lying on the floor in there, forever waiting for whatever little kid dropped it to come back.

I don't want to think of that.

The tall office buildings on Main and King Streets are laddered with long-fingered vines, and birds fly in and out of the shattered windows spotting the sides. It's not really safe to walk there anymore, unless I keep to the other side of the street, because other things are breaking up there too. About six months ago I was nearly brained by a hunk of brick that fell from somewhere high up on the bank building.

The old church on 3rd Street is nearly smothered in flowering vine, the blooms a pale lily white. I went in once; a few months after The Event, not long after I'd satisfied myself that I really was the only one left. The light from the stained-glass windows made pretty colored wedges on the floor. There was a huge Bible left open on the lectern next to the altar. I remember peering down at it in the dim light, at chapters and verses, the clearest words I'd ever seen, I am the Alpha and the Omega, the beginning and the end.

I haven't gone in since. It was too echoey, and the roof has started falling in. It's dangerous. I could die.

I always make sure I'm home before it gets dark. Between the dying streetlights along the way back, and the roaming dog packs, I want to be inside before nightfall. Besides, I don't like walking past all the lightless houses.

I lock the doors out of habit, water the plants, and make dinner. The walls in the living room are lined with boxes; all the things I've brought home, supplies and entertainment enough for a lifetime. I leave the plate of spaghetti on the coffee table beside the couch, while I sort through DVDs, looking for likely items for a night's viewing. For something to watch, it has to be DVDs now, of course - the TV shows nothing but snow otherwise.

That was one of the things that convinced me everyone really was gone: no TV coming from anywhere, and the radio a smooth band of static on both AM and FM. I remember calling random phone numbers; local, then long-distance, then international, in the weeks after The Event. All I ever got was either endless, senseless ringing, or answering machines. I even left messages on some of them, incoherent and shaky, asking anyone who ever heard it to please call back.

Nobody ever did.

The Internet went permanently still at precisely 5:57 pm that June 22nd, too. I spent weeks roaming it for hours at a time, looking for any sign that anybody, anywhere, had posted anything after that time and date, sending RSVP messages to complete strangers on roughly fifty million message boards. No one ever answered any of those, either. It was the Internet silence, more than anything else, which finally convinced me that I was alone. Interestingly, I can still bring up a lot of things on the computer here at home, although some of the big search engines and a lot of little sites have disappeared. Probably whatever servers were hosting them failed since The Event.

I haven't gone online in a long time, though. The stillness of it, an electronic fly in amber, is too strange.

I find something among the DVDs that looks interesting - a season box set of one of my favorite shows - and settle down to watch it. Rain is tapping fitfully against the windows. I keep all my attention on the TV, not even bothering to get up and wash the spaghetti plate.

The DVDs are to remind me. This is how people looked, how they moved and gestured, how voices sounded in a conversation.

My own memories are so dim now.

Sometimes I dream that it never happened. That I wake up to the sound of Dad rattling around in the kitchen, watch the morning news, head off to school in a bus that weaves through traffic, and spend a day amid the racket of two thousand fellow students. When I wake up from those dreams, I stare at the ceiling a long time, preserving for a little while the illusion that I'll step outside into the world the way it used to be. The world the way it would still be, if my focus with the box that day had been clearer.

I think I've adjusted though. Mostly. This new morning, I remember where and what I am from the beginning.

I eat some cornflakes, pack my dance bag, and grab an umbrella for the trip to the dance studio. It's still raining, the sky filled with snarling gray. Ever since The Event, it's rained a lot more often. Maybe the absence of people and everything they dumped into the atmosphere has done something to the weather patterns.

The studio is cool and dim. I stretch, put on a red leotard and a little red skirt, tie pointe shoes, and then go to the west-facing window and pull the blind up, leaving the glass unobstructed.

I turn and see myself, reflected over and over in all the mirrors on the walls, the open window and the city skyline just across the river showing behind me. The view is fuzzed with rain, but I can still see the buildings in the reflections, dark and full of holes and blurred with the vines looking to cover them and bring them down.

Somewhere outside, close by but still faint, I hear a crunching, brief crash. Another roof falling in, someplace in the surrounding area. It doesn't matter. It wouldn't, unless it was at home or here at the studio. I put the music on, the score from

Giselle this time.

There isn't much that matters left at all. If it's not of immediate importance to me, it's of no importance to anyone on Earth. Literally. It's not important if a roof falls, or a building, or a city. It hasn't even turned out to matter much that I murdered billions, instead of murdering just Bianca Rahm, because I didn't take the time to form a specific enough mental image.

Everything is just fine without them. And when I'm gone too, the world will be fine without any of us.

Pirouette.

Arabesque.

Plié. Plié. Plié.

In the time between, I get to be the best dancer in the world.

Lazy Ear
Matthew Damprie

He was the only white kid in class. His hair was jelled and combed forward over his eyes. He drew pentagrams on his notebooks and forearms with a red grading pen I gave him one day when he forgot his pencil. He seldom participated in classroom activities and never spoke so much as a word to any of the other kids. I never called his parents. I admired the way he feverishly scrawled into his composition books. He filled each of them with an endless red paragraph of the most shocking handwriting. Every letter appeared to be in anguish.

He was operating under the mistaken impression that everyone was against him. The truth was that he was a dirty white kid and no one cared about him. He wasn't part of their hierarchy. Most of the white kids were mentally disturbed or mentally disabled or both. He had a lisp and his tongue usually budded through a hole left by a chipped tooth in his nervous grin. For all of the anti-everything he preached his taste in clothes and movies and music was less than far reaching. All of the metal bands he liked were ones you've heard of and his shirts could all be found at discount department stores.

If anything made the black kids wary of him it was the idea that he practiced devil worship in his spare time. This is not something that the African American community tolerates. He made me uneasy, but I can't say it was because I thought he dabbled in the Satan worship. One of his ears was misshapen. You could tell that his hairstyle was a futile attempt to disguise it. No manner of long hair could cover that ear. This might explain why the school's policy on hats was a major point of contention for him. He would wear a black beanie right up to the metal detectors everyday where one of the football coaches would make him take it off. He always ripped it off his head dramatically and shoved it into his bag, defeated.

After seventh hour on Fridays, he could be seen in the hallway pulling the beanie down over that wandering ear and if anyone said anything to him he would say, "School's over!" and that would be that because no teacher in their right mind would waste an unpaid minute following him down to the buses.

During class when the kids were done with their work, I would walk around the room to look busy for any prying eyes that might stop by to rate my teaching performance. I would work my way around the room and try to see what it was the kid was scribbling in his notebook. He would sense this and adjust his shoulders accordingly. One morning, I was fortunate that he had a nose bleed. In the midst of one of his vicious writing sessions, when he seemed to be channeling some unearthly power, he got up suddenly and pointed to the door. I nodded for him to go. The kids all looked sickened and distracted so I told them,

"You're not getting AIDS. Get back to work."

The hour ended before the kid made it back for his things. It was my plan period, so after the class filed out I locked the door and shut off the lights so no one would come by to make small talk or ask me for a favor. There it was, spattered in black blood – the notebook. I put on a pair of latex-free gloves provided by the school nurse in the event that a blood borne pathogen should be avoided.

I gently lifted the cover and peered inside. There were the usual pentagrams and upside down crosses drawn in the margins. One page contained an ambitious portrait of Satan with breasts. He sat in a chair with his legs crossed, poised with a pen and paper. The piece was entitled, The True Mother. Underneath it was the phrase HEAR NO EVIL, with the word, NO, crossed out.

What followed was a boring account of a pitiful childhood I initially mistook for his, until the story detailed a college experience and grim job search not unlike my own. The writing went on to describe my current existential crisis, including the bit about walking around the room to look busy.

Someone was banging on the door like a SWAT team. I carefully closed the journal and returned it to its exact position at the kid's desk. Some of the blood droplets had run but I hoped he would mistake this for velocity spatter. There he was, outside the small rectangular window of glass and chicken wire, with wads of tissue twisted up his nostrils. I let him in. He gathered up his things without a word and left.

I spent the rest of my plan period pretending to grade things as I contemplated the events that had just occurred. I went to the bathroom, which reeked of weed, and wiped my face with wet paper towels. There was half a joint in the urinal and I smoked it after carefully checking the hallway. I could feel a panic attack coming on. I smoked it down and sat in the dark of my classroom for another half hour before the next group of kids came in.

I was feeling good now. I had some fun with the writing prompt. It was, Do you ever have the feeling that someone is reading your mind? The kids had some great stories and I asked about them all in detail. I even sent a girl down to the vending machines to bring me back a Dr. Pepper, which is something only the fat teachers ever do.

I had a weekly appointment required by the school district. The psychiatrist's office was an unimpressive structure across from the Dairy Queen in the old part of our tiny downtown. It shared a parking lot with a church whose Christian daycare staff was highly suspicious of any grown man sitting in his car waiting for a session.

The office was converted from a small home where the once green grass had been draped in a thick black blanket of asphalt. The whole place had the look of a roadside antique shop. The waiting room was furnished with an assortment of square, wooden, padded chairs – the kind you would find in a public library. They were damp-smelling and upholstered with a tattered green fabric patterned with the shapes of small leaves and berries – likely some Christmas fabric purchased at a discount some January. I unwillingly sat down and waited my turn. I was unable to make out any words but a woman went on and on about something in the other room, separated only by a short hallway.

The session ended ten minutes late and when the woman came into the waiting room I avoided eye contact. The psychiatrist took her time with the woman's payment and after an extended conversation about scheduling, she finally left.

The room where my therapy sessions were held was small and decorated only by coloring pages ripped haphazardly from cheap supermarket books and taped to the wall. Most of her clients were children.

We sat at identical chairs with a restored wooden chest between us that served as a coffee table. There were Crayons and a pair of safety scissors at my feet.

"How are you feeling?" she asked.

"Unwell," I told her after a pause.

"Why is that?" she questioned.

"There's something happening to me." I watched her carefully for an eye roll, but there was none. She was good.

"Fill me in."

"There's a boy in my class. He knows things about me."

"What kinds of things?"

"Details about my life. My background. My thoughts."

"Do you think he's digging through your trash?" She smiled.

"No."

"A diary maybe – one you left at school by mistake?"

"No. It's not like that. These aren't things I've written down. These aren't things that can be looked up in the yellow pages." I leaned forward to whisper, fearful that the next client in line was eavesdropping on me. "This boy, he makes these strange drawings in his notebooks. Everything is devil worship with him. It's like he's stumbled onto something and now he's listening to me think while he should be doing his homework. He's writing this story – he's filled up a couple of notebooks and today he left the room and I was able to read a page or two."

"And you think what you read resembles your life?"

"To a tee."

"It's not uncommon for someone to read something and see their face reflected in it."

I sat back and quit whispering. "It's not a reflection. It's a goddamn portrait."

"Why don't you entertain the idea that all of this could be the result of some underlying issue?"

"Like what?"

"Could it be that you have some anxiety about your privacy? Coming here and telling me about your thoughts

– your background – could be causing you to manifest the stress you feel in the form of some outside force. It's a way for your mind to deal with new and confusing emotions." She saw the underwhelmed look on my face. "Give it a week. Come back here in one week and tell me I'm wrong. Give it a week."

She smiled.

I left.

I spent the weekend researching the dark arts. This didn't help my anxiety. I checked the windows repeatedly. There may have been someone out there – the kid maybe – watching the house. Maybe he was out there getting my poor brain in range of his misshapen ear.

Hearing my thoughts.

I tried to think of nothing. I cleared my mind. I meditated. I tried to read, watch a movie, do anything besides air out my thoughts. It was no use. If he was to continue putting this hex on me, I was an open book.

Then came Monday.

I wanted to come into class that day and be assured that I had manifested the whole thing, but that's not what happened. The kid had apparently gone on some kind of macabre shopping spree at one of those gothic stores at the mall. His pant legs were so wide they covered his pen scribbled shoes. A long black hoodie hung from his shoulders, pulled tight on his head by fists jammed into the kangaroo pocket. The chain from his wallet hung as low as his knees. It was made from interlocking skulls.

His face was a mass distraction. Eyeliner was poorly applied. Likely he had put it on while riding the bus. None of the kids looked at him. They sensed the validation he so craved and thus deprived him of it. My casual gawking was not enough to satisfy his hunger. Adults were easy to disgust. His body arched over when he moved across the room, like he had been taught to walk in a crawl space.

He took his seat in the back and pulled out The Book. How many more chapters had he written about me over the weekend? How many volumes did he have at home? Were they organized by time or subject? Could I ever peruse the library of my own mind? He began to write even before I put the prompt up on the board.

"Quiet, please. Quiet!" I waited for them to shut up. "Write about a time that you knew something you shouldn't." I stood over the kid, straining my eyes to read what he etched there.

"Like what?" a girl asked. They all seemed engaged. This was rare, so I spoke in low tones for effect.

"A secret," I said. "Something you found out that you weren't ever supposed to know."

"Like yo mamma was cheatin'?" a boy that never talked before said.

"Just like that," I said.

The kids all began to write, except for Him. He just sat there with his palms on the table, staring at the wall in disgust.

He looked sick. I watched him from across the room, pretending to check on other students' progress. His eyes flicked back into his head. He began to convulse and scrabble at his throat.

Was he choking? None of the kids would look at him.

He made some deep grunting sounds and brought up a wad of something in a pool of white liquid.

I walked to him slowly.

He took the pellet from the puddle of milk-white vomit and opened it up slowly. I stood there above him, ignored. It was a sheet of notebook paper.

He smoothed it out.

There among the blue and red lines was a drawing of my face. He wiped the liquid from it and I could see four words there scrawled above my head.

GIVE IT A WEEK, they read.

I stumbled through the hallway not knowing where I would go. For a long time, I've had this fantasy about leaving work one day and stripping off all of my clothes to walk down the highway.

I kicked off my shoes and unbuttoned my shirt. I left them behind me. I was dying. I couldn't breathe. They would fire me for sure. Kids looked out from the rectangle windows now. Their gossip traveled faster than I could crawl. I was making noise now. Gasping for breath. Maybe I was screaming. The school nurse found me and dragged me into her room.

"Breathe," she said. She really hated having her day interrupted by things like this. I took a breath in and sent fifteen back out. "You've having another panic attack. You need to breathe." Her walkie-talkie was alive with questions. She covered for me. While I gasped between my knees she went and grabbed my shirt and shoes. She called the lounge and got some teacher on their break to watch my kids. I could speak again.

"Vomit," was all I said. She handed me a trashcan. "No," I said and pushed it away. "A boy in my class. Vomit on his desk."

She called down to the room. "Nobody sick?" she said. "A white kid." She looked at me. "Not there?" she said and hung up.

"Not there?" I asked.

"Not there."

"He left."

"And the vomit?"

"He probably mopped it up with his goddamn triple extra large hoodie."

I closed my eyes and lay in the dark for what seemed like a long time. The nurse brought me an Aspirin and a Dixie Cup of water. She was looking at my medical emergency contact card.

"Do you need me to call your appointed therapist?"

"No. Look the boy up. I'm calling his parents." She backed into her office and turned down the easy listening station on her radio. I sat up to tie my shoes and button my dress shirt.

"I'm confused," she said when she came back out. She had a medical emergency contact card in each hand.

"What is it?" I stood up and pushed in my shirttail.

"His mother has the same name as your psychiatrist."

I drove up the highway possessed. My hands shook. I grinded my teeth. I imagined that I could see myself walking the center line like a tightrope – naked. I swerved and made roadkill of that desperate fantasy. I weaved through cars. I followed too closely. I changed lanes without signaling. I was driving like everyone else. We were all on our way somewhere to make someone pay. We were destroying the time it took to get there.

The Dairy Queen sign. The daycare. Her office.

I let myself in. I would kick down the doors, I thought. Drag the person out who was taking my spot. There was no need. She was there waiting for me.

"Your school's nurse called." I didn't say a word. "Another panic attack?" I shook my head at her. We went in and sat at the identical chairs. The same pile of Crayons lay at my feet. From between the hinges of the coffee table trunk hung a few links of a familiar chain. As she readied her notebook I pinched the interlocking skulls between my thumb and forefinger.

"What brings you back so early?" she asked.

"I wanted to tell you something," I said.

"Ok."

"I realized something today." I glanced back down at the chain. The links clicked quietly into the trunk, one by one. "It just hit me. You're right. You've been right all along."

"About what exactly?"

"Everything."

She laughed.

"I'm a cured man. I won't be coming to see you anymore." She looked more entertained than concerned.

"Is that right?"

"That's right." She looked at me for a long time.

"Well can I give you something?" She rose and went to her desk to dig around. I reached around the trunk and secured the latch. I turned the key and put it in my pocket. She came back and handed me a pendant. It was a scorpion under acrylic glass. The back was engraved. It read, THE ONLY SAFE WAY TO HOLD A SCORPION. "I found this at a gift shop some time ago and it reminded me of you. I didn't know how you'd take it."

"Am I the scorpion?"

"You're the glass," she said. I stood up so we could awkwardly shake hands before I left.

The kid wasn't at school the rest of that week. He never came back. His mother reported him missing. The nurse kept our strange coincidence to herself. "Did you see the news?" she asked me one morning. "They found that kid from your class inside his mother's trunk."

"Really," I said.

"Poor thing, she told the police he would try to sneak in during her sessions."

"You don't say."

"They said she didn't find him until the smell came. She had no idea where it was coming from. Called an exterminator to find a dead rat in the walls and found her boy curled up in a trunk."

"Imagine that."

"Have you gone to see her recently?"

"No. I'm cured."

It was early so I sat in my classroom with the lights off waiting for the sun to rise, and for the kids to come riding their wave of profanity up the hall. I looked at the kid's desk. There was a symbol written in permanent marker on the side. An arrow pointing down. I leaned down and glanced beneath it.

Something was written there.

I flipped the desk and turned on the lights. There was a note. The handwriting was even more unusual than usual. It was as though he had written it slowly, without looking.

It read, MOTHER PUTS ME IN A TRUNK SO I WILL LISTEN AND LEARN. SHE SAYS I'VE GOT A LAZY EAR.

Second Hand Books

A. Gregg

Of all the little things in life that brought Rachel immense joy, finding signs of other people's lives in second hand books was her absolute favourite. Just this week she'd so far marvelled at a flyer for a reggae festival that had happened a decade ago but still looked great fun. She'd started a new book yesterday and was already half-way through it, having been gripped early on and staying up far later than intended and indeed was sensible before a long working day. Rachel concealed a yawn and leant over the counter of the nurse's station to check that the old man in his pyjamas shuffling towards the loo was steady enough on his feet. He took a hand off his Zimmer frame to wave genially at her and she nodded encouragingly, knowing it would take him five minutes to walk down a short corridor that she could complete in a few strides. She also knew he wouldn't accept her help and that he didn't particularly need it. 'No harm in taking things at a slower pace,' Rachel thought to herself, looking forward to the end of her shift even though it wasn't for hours. She had a stern word with herself about needing to learn to put down books at a sensible time and went to make some coffee.

When she got home that night she went straight to bed and resisted picking up the book, knowing that no matter how tired she was if she tried to read just one page to relax her mind it would turn into hours of wide and glassy eyed literary involvement. It turned out she didn't need to lull herself to an appropriate state of calm and she noted that she was smiling at the thought of her book addiction in the last moment before she was soundly asleep.

Soon though her sleep was troubled, and in her rapid dreams Rachel gasped for air, willing herself to wake from the scenes that flashed before her mind's eye before she got a chance to put her finger on what they were, knowing only that they scared her and she wanted more than anything to escape from them. She awoke with a cry and a gasp, sitting up straight in bed and wondering for a sleep-furred moment if she'd fallen asleep sitting up reading. The dream fog trailed away and she remembered falling asleep quickly and the only trace of her dreams was a lingering exhaustion that she knew she wouldn't be able to shake all day.

Rachel managed to resist lying flat out on the counter of the nurse's station and snoozing. After what seemed like a week's worth of staying awake in one long shift and after more coffees than she could keep track of, as well as numerous weak smiles at the old man as he made his way back and forth along the corridor, it was finally, blessedly, time for home again. She managed to stay awake on the public transport, acknowledging that even though it was painful to her weary body to stand and balance and avoid elbows, at least she was too uncomfortable to fall asleep on a stranger's shoulder and embarrass herself with snoring in public and dribbling on a city boy's expensive shirt. Dragging herself the few streets from the station to her flat she thought only of her bed and not at all of her book.

Feeling like she'd achieved a mission akin to mountain climbing simply by summoning up the energy to brush her teeth, Rachel rushed gratefully under the duvet and was fast asleep before she'd even finished nestling it around her shoulders.

Her sleep was deep, her ears unhearing to any of the cars or drunken shouts or fighting cats outside. She knew only the sensation of her throat tightening, of being unable to scream, of images of shaking hands encroaching on her vision. She awoke suddenly, trembling and grateful to the police siren in the deep night that had disturbed her. Taking a few deep breaths, Rachel forced herself to think about what had been running through her nightmares.

With the lamp on, the fear faded and although a tingle went up her spine as she pictured those shaking hands, she remembered that she'd spent most of the last fortnight keeping an unobtrusive eye out for the stability of the old man on her ward. In fact, now that she thought about it, she was the one who'd been consuming gallons of coffee for the past couple of days; it was only surprising that she'd dreamed of shaky hands and not needing to pee. She got up and went to the bathroom, and returned to sleep without remembering her dreams.

Rachel woke with a jolt, panicked and without

a sense of time and place. A moment went by and she recalled who she was, and with even greater relief, that the alarm hadn't gone off because it was her day off. She drew back the curtains to watch the outside world go about its business in the cold grey streets, and allowing herself a small smug smile she drew the curtains again and got back into bed.

She read and she dozed and she read and she dozed and it was on page 101 that Rachel saw the thumbprint. She gazed at it respectfully, feeling a bond with this person who had read the book before her, maybe last week, maybe decades ago. She compared her own thumb pad on top of it; enjoying being able to work out it was a man because it was significantly bigger than hers. She gave it an affectionate smile, turned the page and carried on with the story. Rachel dozed. She had no idea what time it was in the real world and even less of an idea in the dream world. She tried to fight through the words that were spinning and blurring then wished she hadn't when she saw the hands, steady now, determined, reach for her.

Rachel screamed and woke herself up. 'Jeez woman,' she told herself, aloud, to hear a voice, 'You need a holiday.' Exhaling, she reached for her book in the hope of not thinking about her dreams. A few more pages, and there were four fingerprints on the side of the page, peeping over and firmly gripping. 'How odd,' thought Rachel. 'No-one holds books like that.' She stared, disconcerted, until the thought occurred to her that maybe someone had been holding the book up for someone else. The fingerprints probably belonged to a health care worker, someone like her, someone who'd patiently held the book for someone who needed assistance and escapism. Feeling much better about the world, Rachel snuggled down and dozed some more.

It was immediate this time. No sooner had she shut her eyes than she was launched into a misty place of nothing but fear and the hands, those hands, brushing against her neck and holding firmly and-

Rachel woke. She just refused, absolutely refused, to be freaked out by a dream. A mere dream. It was, in fact, a cheek that her lovely dream time was being so rudely interfered with by this insubordinate of a collection of thoughts that she hadn't actually even thought in the first place thank you very much. Good. That had told that. She have the general air around her a haughty nod to show that she'd tolerate no more of this nonsense, and picked up her book so that the immediate world in general knew it was being chastened. Rachel looked down to start to read and before she had time to register what she saw, the hand prints lifted off the page and wrapped themselves around her neck. Her final thought was how she wished she could have disappeared into the world of the reggae festival instead, and then she was no more- just a smudge, in a tale, that will be passed on...

Author Bios:

Raven Black Unknown

Charlotte Birch Charlotte lives in a small town in Shropshire, England. She is a full time writer with a Master's Degree in Creative Writing. Her favourite genres to write in our horror, thrillers and science fiction.

Matthew C. Dampier is a short story author and songwriter who resides in Kansas City, Missouri. When he isn't entertaining his wife and young child, he occupies himself with the absurd and macabre.

A.Gregg A.Gregg is a London based writer who works in print, radio, stage and screen. She specialises in comedy, horror, and deciding whether to put a comma before 'and'

Steven Spellman Steven Spellman is a 32 year old career writer living in North Carolina with his beautiful wife and two gorgeous daughters. The only thing that comes close to being as important to him as his family is his passion for writing. His newest novel I have a novel out, *The Virus* can be found at bookstores

J.B. Wiliams J.B. Williams is a writer and editor living near Atlanta, Georgia, with a spouse, six cats, and roughly three thousand books.

Also Available:

Book 1: The Catacombs, Tales of the Bizarre and Twisted

Book 2: The Catacombs, Short Stories of Horror and Misery

Book 3: The Catacombs, Enter the Dark

Book 4: The Catacombs, The Unknown

If you are interested in submitting a story for

consideration for the next edition of

The Catacombs

email: Submissions@gauthierpublications.com

The Sound of Ice
by J.B. Williams

We saw the sun for the last time today. Hayes told us what to expect. There will be a faint glow on the horizon for a few days, marking the spot where the sun is, and then nothing for three months. Only moon, stars, and the aurora australis. Worth is happy; the darkness will serve his astronomical observations well.

We found the old hut from Armstrong's Endeavour expedition in good shape. The only problem was that the door had been ripped from its hinges. The poor devils probably left it open accidentally the day they set out and never returned, and the winds did the rest. Dare fixed it, with a few choice words for

The ship has already left the harbor. Wished them luck on their sea studies. The pack ice is forming. I got a fire started in the blubber stove. Hayes and Dare are at the table, arguing some prehistoric geology points I don't understand three words of. Worth is asleep, snoring like a train. Cozy in here, even with the wind.

29 April

Awakened around 3 a.m. by ungodly screeching and hissing. Dare awoke to find something furry draped over his face, and leapt from his bunk shouting. It was the ship's cat, Aurora. Hayes found one of our spare bags chewed open.

87

Suspect she climbed in aboard the ship, fell asleep, and then came out after nightfall. Pity we can't contact the ship; they'll be wondering what happened to her. She's sitting in front of the stove right now, washing up - luckily we have fish she can eat!

Today Hayes and I hiked up the coast. There's an Emperor penguin rookery a little ways east. Collection of egg specimens - possibly even photography with the use of the flash boxes - would be an accomplishment.

On the way back, kept hearing an odd sound: hissing and faint bubbling on the snow-drowned hills above. Rather like the sound of the ship's boiler. Unsure what it might be here.

Worth and Dare worked past midnight setting up telescopic and magnetic measuring equipment. I nearly have my lab as I want it. Hayes actually cooked dinner without burning it - and some say miracles no longer happen!

1 MAY

The first of the auroras came: great rippling curtains of bright green mist fanning across the black sky. It was bright enough to light up the hills behind the cape and make the snow gleam. Also gave us some welcome illumination out on the ice. The air has a peculiar crackly feel when an aurora is in full bloom. Worth checks his instruments and speculates on the possibility of auroras generating static electricity. By "speculates" I mean muttering his thoughts aloud endlessly till some other member of the party pleads for silence!

There are large veins of copper in the earth here. They're visible in the aurora-light, pale green webs in the rock near the beach. Worth thinks they're interfering with his equipment.

He keeps registering readings from much nearer the ground.
Dare says the Canadian Natives have stories about auroras "singing". Probably some very faint sound generated high in the atmosphere, and in the clear still cold of polar nights, it's audible at ground level. That might explain hearing the high

hissing and bubbling sounds again. Closer to the hut this time - it would be stronger, given the aurora's intensity. Hayes disagrees and wonders about small volcanic vents in the area. If there is volcanism anywhere near, I hope it holds its peace.

5 MAY

Worth just returned from going uphill to collect ice for water. Eyes bugging out of his head, babbling. "Ground auroras, never thought this was possible!" After we sat him down and got him a smoke, he continued with an iota more calm.

While he was chopping out ice for the buckets, he heard that bubbling hiss we associated with the big auroras. Coming from all directions, he said. He looked up and saw "queer flat lights, green like the sky auroras, but moving along the ground in a sort of swarm." They zigzagged and then came toward him. He grabbed the buckets and ran. He swears the lights followed him and actually shot out a tendril that wrapped around his right ankle for a moment.

Dare looked at Worth's right foot, and then went very pale. "Did you notice this?" he said, and pointed.

Worth's boot and sock were cut clean through all round, in a neat circle. He bent over, the pipe still in his mouth, and removed them. There was an odd blackish-green discoloration ringing his ankle. It's not a bruise, but not exactly a burn, either.

END OF PREVIEW